Tina Tuff! What a name! How could any parent with half a brain call their kid Tina Tuff?

Ever since I was little, people have told me that I'm tough. Tough Tina Tuff! I have to live up to my name.

Tina is tough all right. But is she tough enough to cope with Granny Tuff?

There is a glossary on page 87 explaining the meaning of some of the Australian terms and sayings that Tina and her friends use.

To my dad, who taught me the true meaning of "tough"

TINA TUFF

Margaret Clark

with illustrations by
Lin Tobias

Cover illustration by
Wendy Smith

Hippo

Scholastic Children's Books,
Scholastic Publications Ltd,
7-9 Pratt Street, London NW1 0AE, UK

Scholastic Inc.,
739 Broadway, New York, NY 10003, USA

Scholastic Canada Ltd,
123 Newkirk Road, Richmond Hill,
Ontario, Canada L4C 3G5

Ashton Scholastic Pty Ltd,
PO Box 579, Gosford, New South Wales,
Australia

Ashton Scholastic Ltd,
Private Bag 1, Penrose, Auckland,
New Zealand

First published in Australia in 1991 by Omnibus Books,
part of the ASHTON SCHOLASTIC GROUP

First published in the UK by Scholastic Publications Ltd, 1994

ISBN: 0 590 55511 1

10 9 8 7 6 5 4 3 2 1

Contents

1

Tina

Tina Tuff! What a name! How could any parent with half a brain call their kid Tina Tuff?

Ever since I was little, people have told me that I'm tough. Tough Tina Tuff! I have to live up to my name.

My two brothers, Tommy and Randy, are tough. Tommy is sixteen, and smart as a tack. He will run this country one day. Randy is a hunk. Girls think he is sexy. He is fourteen and built like King Kong.

I am eleven years old. I look tough. I have this spiky haircut with orange streaks. Mum yells a lot about this, but I take no notice. I get to wear Tommy or Randy's shirts, socks, and earrings. Mum yells a lot about that, too. I've told her that I'm saving up for a tattoo. That freaks her right out.

I guess my mum is tough in her own way, although she is tiny and rather feminine. My dad, that is, my real dad, got killed in a car accident when I was six. Mum was doing OK bringing us up by herself, even though we were all a bit on the wild side. Then she met this creep, Mr Donald Donaldson. What a name! He wants me to call him Dad. Actually he wanted me to call him Dad straight after the wedding ceremony, which I didn't want to attend. I really carried on about it, but I still had to go. That was six months ago, and I still hate Mr Donald Donaldson. I won't call him Dad. No way! He can't replace my dad. I don't want him around!

I act tough. I have to act tough and look tough 'cos I am the head of my gang. The Coucals. Any money you don't know what a coucal is. Well, it's this super tough bird. It's brown and shiny, with this mean, curved beak. It lives in Africa. And it can survive almost anything. Just like me. I didn't want a dopey name for our gang, like Gremlins or Venom Vendors or Raiders. I wanted a name that no one else would have in the whole of Australia. The Coucals. It suits our gang. I wrote "Coucals Rule" on the school wall with chalk. Someone dobbed. Boy, did I cop it. Did I care?

So. To be in my gang you have to be cool. Not a wimp. Most of the kids at my school want to be in the Coucals. I'm not sexist. Boys can be in the gang. We have Rod, Ben, Ziggie, Pigman, and Frankie. The girls are Sharon, Lisa, Zena, and Eva. At school we hang out at the corner shed, or in the middle of the oval, so we can see the teachers coming. After school we hang out at the milk bar until 5 pm.

To get into the gang you have to pass a test. It's like a dare. There's an old saying, "He who dares,

wins." That's our motto for the Coucals. I like that motto.

This new kid at our school wanted to join the Coucals. He didn't have a hope. For a start, he was a real nerd. His name was William Wormley. We called him The Worm. He was definitely not Coucal material.

"Get lost, Worm," I said, when he came up to us in the school yard.

"Yeah. Rack off back to your hole," said Frankie.

Clever!

"Can I join your gang?" asked The Worm. "Just give me a dare and I'll do it."

"Next loser," said Zena, yawning.

"Forget it," I said. "We don't need a worm in the Coucals. Coucals eat worms, don't you know that, Willie Worm?"

This kid had a problem like I did. His name. He was supposed to act like a worm. Same as I was supposed to act tough. Didn't that kid know *anything*?

The Worm kept on nagging. He knew how to nag. He was even worse than Mr Donald Donaldson, and that's saying something. He kept on and on and on until Rod socked him one on the nose. But still he wouldn't take no for an answer.

"OK," I said, fed up, "here's the dare. You have to climb up on to the school roof. In broad daylight. You have to spray 'Teachers stink. Coucals rule' in big writing on each building. Big enough so that when we stand on Nob Hill we can read it clearly. Big enough so that a jet pilot can see it. I dare you."

"Right," said The Worm. "I'll do it. Then I can be in the gang."

Good one! What if he did it? Then he would be in the Coucals. We did not want a wimp in the Coucals.

"And another thing," I said. "You know those stupid roller-skates you have, instead of a skateboard like all the other kids? You have to wear your roller-skates when you do it!"

"On your feet, not tied around your neck," said Pigman.

"OK," said The Worm, "I'll wear my roller-skates on my feet when I spray the roof. Anything else?"

"Yeah," I said. "No clothes except your jocks."

It was the middle of winter. The Worm would freeze to death before he had time to start writing.

"OK," said The Worm, "I'll spray the roof wearing roller-skates and my jocks."

What was he, nuts or something?

"It will be at lunchtime," I said, "so every kid in the school can see you."

"OK," said The Worm, "I'll wear my roller-skates on my feet when I spray 'Teachers stink, Coucals rule' on each roof in my jocks at lunchtime. And then I'll be in the Coucals."

No way. We could always change our minds.

We set it up for Thursday. The Worm had to provide the spray can, his roller-skates and his jocks. We had to provide the audience. No problems. Every kid in the school knew about the dare in no time.

Thursday arrived, windy and cold. Luckily it wasn't raining. Or unluckily, 'cos then we could have called off the dare. Two teachers were on duty at lunchtime. Ben and Eva were going to keep one teacher busy by dobbing on kids, and Frankie would fake a broken arm on the oval to keep the other teacher busy. The Coucals were giving The Worm a fighting chance.

The Worm stripped to his jocks. Can you believe pale blue, with red hearts? Off! On went his roller-skates. He had black paint in a spray can. He looked a real nerd.

The Worm shinned up the drainpipe. It wasn't easy with roller-skates on, but he made it. He rolled across one roof. We could see him using the spray can. I should have made the dare much harder. If The Worm succeeded, we'd have every dork in the school trying to join the Coucals.

"Hey, you!" yelled Mrs Walsgott, the Grade 5 teacher, coming out the door.

We'd forgotten the noise that the roller-skates would make on the school roof. Clackety-clack. More teachers came spilling out the doors.

"Get off the roof!" roared Mrs Walsgott.

Mr Creedy, the other Grade 5 teacher, started to climb up the drainpipe. He was short and fat.

The drainpipe was long and skinny. Oh, *best*. Perhaps he'd fall off. He'd been my teacher the year before, and he was a real pig. No one liked him. Every kid in the school was watching. This was fun.

The Worm rolled over the roof. He had to get across to the next roof. He took a flying leap. The kids gaped. The teachers gaped. He missed the next roof. The spray can came bouncing down ... *splat!* Black paint flew everywhere. The Worm hung on to the guttering, his legs scrambling for a foothold. He couldn't do it with roller-skates tacked to his feet. The guttering started to sag.

"Quick! Give me your hand!" shouted Mr Creedy, who had made it safely to the other roof.

This was better than late-night television.

"Get a ladder!" screamed Mrs Walsgott.

Too late. The Worm grabbed at Mr Creedy's pudgy paw—and missed. The guttering gave way. *Crash! Splat!* The Worm lay in a pool of black paint. Was he dead? I felt sick. He was so still. Had my dad looked like that when he got killed? Was it my fault that William Wormley was dead? I didn't mean for him to fall and die.

"Is he all right?" asked Mr Dans, my Grade teacher.

The Worm was lying at a funny angle. He didn't seem to be breathing.

"Don't move him," called Mr Creedy from the roof. He's supposed to be a first aid expert. "Call an ambulance."

The ambulance came screaming up to the school. So did heaps of parents. They thought something chronic had happened to their kids. Naturally my mum and Mr Donald Donaldson didn't come screaming up. They were both at work. Mum didn't like getting called up to schools, 'cos it usually meant that Tommy, Randy or I were in trouble again.

The Worm groaned as the ambulancemen lifted him on to a stretcher. He opened his eyes and looked straight at me. *Alive.* Huh! "Does this mean I can't be in the Coucals?" he asked.

How dumb is dumb? Did we need a loser like The Worm in the Coucals?

"You failed," I said. "You did not finish the dare. You definitely cannot join the Coucals."

The Worm looked really bad, but no way was I going to let him see that I was upset.

The ambulancemen pushed me aside and loaded The Worm into the ambulance. The teachers started asking kids questions but they knew better than to spill their guts. The Coucals would get them if they did.

We all went up to Nob Hill after school. We couldn't wait to see if The Worm had written anything, and if we could read it. We could. The whole city could. There on the roof we saw: TEACHERS RULE. COUCALS STINK. Stupid nerd. He'd messed it up. That was it, for sure. The Worm would never be in the Coucals! Ever!

When I got home Mum went berko, and so did

Mr Donald Donaldson. Some twerp had dobbed on the Coucals. The principal had phoned. All the Coucals' parents had to pay to get the roof repainted. The teachers were in a real panic about getting the writing covered up with new paint. At least that was good news.

Once I found out who had dobbed on the Coucals, their life wouldn't be worth living. If they were bigger than me I would get Tommy or Randy to punch out their lights.

But worse was still to come. Mr Donald Donaldson, the big creep, said he was sick of me acting tough. It was time I got straightened out. And my mum agreed with him! Firstly, I would get no pocket money for six months. I had to help pay off the roof. And secondly, I was being sent to Granny Tuff's place.

Granny Tuff would get me sorted out, my mum said. Granny Tuff is my real dad's mother. I hadn't seen her since the funeral. Everyone else had been bawling their eyes out at the graveside except Granny Tuff. And me. She was supposed to be Super Tuff.

Granny Tuff lives by herself way out in Woop Woop on a farm near the mountains. I hadn't been there since I was tiny. All I could remember was that it was a rundown old dump, and Granny Tuff was a rundown old frump!

The principal got Mr Dans to give me heaps and heaps of homework. He did it 'cos he hated me! No way was I going to do it.

Staying with Granny Tuff would be the pits. No friends. No Coucals. No money. No fun. This was going to be the worst time of my entire life!

And although I was acting tough, deep inside I was cringing, really scared. What if The Worm *did* cark it? I'd have that on my conscience for the rest of my life!

2

Granny Tuff

Mr Donald Donaldson drove me to Granny Tuff's farm the next day. He wouldn't let my mum drive me in case I talked her out of it. What a slime! I would hate him as long as I lived.

I didn't speak *one word* to him the whole way there, and the trip took four hours. Wait: I tell a lie. When we stopped at a roadside café and he asked if I would like a hamburger and a chocolate thickshake, I nodded. Then he stood with his arms folded until I said, "Yes." "Yes, what?" he said, like teachers do when they want you to say "please". I said, "Yes, I'll have a hamburger and a chocolate thickshake." He gave up and bought me the stuff. My real dad would never have let me get away with such rude behaviour.

My real dad was tough but fair. He took Tommy, Randy and me out camping sometimes, and taught us how to catch fish. He even taught Tommy how to shoot at targets. He went with us to footy matches when Tommy and Randy were in the Little League, and he told us these great stories about when he was a kid on the farm ...

Mr Donald Donaldson was the exact opposite to my real dad. He went to a posh school when he was a kid, in the middle of Sydney. He played tennis. He's never been fishing in his life. My real dad was a motor mechanic, and there was nothing he didn't know about cars. My stepdad doesn't know the first thing about cars; he phones the RACV when our car conks out. He wears a suit to work, which is in some crummy office right in the middle of town. I don't know why my mum ever married rotten, wimpy Mr Donald Donaldson. Still, living with him was one hundred per cent better than going to Granny Tuff's farm. I had to do something!

"Ohhhh," I moaned, holding my stomach.

"What's wrong, Tina? Don't you feel well?"

I groaned again and closed my eyes.

"Perhaps you'd better lie down in the back seat for a while."

He pulled over and stopped the car against the grassy verge. I clambered out, opened the rear door, and climbed into the back, pulling the door shut. I had toyed briefly with the idea of running off into the bushes, but I knew he'd soon have caught me. He'd be sure to run faster than me with his gangly long legs.

We drove off down the highway again. I rummaged in my green bag, the one holding all my schoolbooks, pens and other useless school junk. Cautiously I tore some pages out of my maths homework book. I stuck them together to form a long strip. Then, carefully, using black Texta, I wrote in large letters: I AM BEING KIDNAPPED.

HELP ME!

Where the heck was the Blu-Tack? Right down the bottom of my bag, of course.

"Are you all right back there, Tina?" said my stepdad, peering into the rearvision mirror. Just as well I hadn't put up my sign. I pretended to be asleep. Then, very slowly, I edged myself upright and put the sign along the bottom part of the back window, so he wouldn't see it. I lay down to await developments.

Nothing happened! So I sat up again.

I spent the next half hour signalling to cars that came past. Lots of people stared, but no one

did anything. Perhaps they thought my stepdad was a maniac with a sawn-off shotgun, instead of a wimpy excuse for a real father.

Finally, just as I was getting desperate, this cop car with two policemen in it came screaming up the highway, siren wailing, lights flashing, and signalled Mr Donald Donaldson, mega-nerd, to pull over.

"Help!" I yelled out of the side window. One of the cops drew his pistol. I hit the floor. For all I knew, he might not have passed his shooting exams at the Police Academy.

"What's wrong?" asked my stepdad nervously.

"Was I speeding?"

"Put your hands on the wheel," said the bigger cop.

"Can I see your driving licence, sir?" asked the smaller one.

Mr Donald Donaldson gave a sort of moan. I stuck my head up to see what was happening. My stepdad had one hand on the wheel and the other hand was trying to extract his driving licence from the glove compartment. You can't please everyone.

"Help me!" I squeaked. "This man has kidnapped me. I want to go home to my mother."

Well, it didn't work. In this world adults always believe other adults. The cops radioed our local police station, and the cop there phoned Mum.

Tina Tuff was not being kidnapped by Mr Donald Donaldson.

"If you were my kid, I'd kill you," the bigger cop said to me.

The rest of the trip was boring, so boring that I went to sleep.

I woke just as we were pulling up outside Granny Tuff's farm in the middle of nowhere. There were mountains all around; not another house to be seen. It would make a great site for a gaol. And it was going to be my gaol for two weeks, or until I learned to behave myself, whichever came first.

Granny Tuff's place looked as if it was about to collapse. It was very, very old, so old that the weatherboards had all faded to a ghostly grey. Some of the windows were shut at one end and open at the other, because the foundations had sunk. The veranda sagged in the middle.

Mr Donald Donaldson opened the rickety gate and we straggled up the weed-covered path to the front door. The veranda shuddered and creaked as we walked across it.

"This is like 'The House of Horror' I saw on TV once," I said desperately. "You can't leave me here."

"Don't be foolish, Tina. Granny Tuff will take good care of you."

Oh, yeah?

Mr Donald Donaldson knocked smartly on the door. I could hear someone shuffling up the passage. I expected the door to be opened by a creepy butler saying, "You rang?" like it happens on horror shows.

The door creaked open. This little old lady with straggly, wispy grey hair was standing there. Granny Tuff. We looked at each other.

"Earl's girl," she said. At first I thought she'd said, "Bull's wool." I thought she was nuts. Then I remembered that Earl was my real dad's name. Earl Tuff! It sounded good, heaps better than Donald Donaldson. Earl Tuff was a *man*'s name! A *real* man's name!

Granny Tuff held open the door, beckoning us to follow her. We walked down this gloomy passage which led to the kitchen.

"Tea?" said Granny Tuff, lifting a sputtering kettle from an ancient black wood stove. It seemed that she was a woman of few words. Good. She might stay off my case.

We sat at this sturdy pine table bleached white with years of scrubbing and scouring, drinking hot tea from blue-and-white-patterned cups with gold crinkly edges. Granny Tuff produced a plate of golden scones, with thick cream and home-made jam. I passed. Cream gives me zits.

Where were the potato crisps? Where was the icy cold Coke?

After a cup of tea and three scones, Mr Donald Donaldson kindly decided to scram. I think Granny Tuff and her home, sweet home were making him nervous. He is strictly a plastic sort of person. I didn't bother to return his wave as he drove off down the road. I was neither glad nor sad to see him go. I'd try my luck with Granny Tuff.

I turned to see her looking at me with sharp, beady eyes.

"You don't like your stepfather," she said matter-of-factly.

He didn't like *me*, did he? Didn't say when, even *if*, he'd be back!

"No," I said.

She nodded. "I'll show you to your room."

I lugged my case and bag of schoolbooks back down the passage. Granny Tuff opened a door. My new bedroom, except "new" couldn't describe it. Because the windows didn't shut properly, cold air swirled through the room like an icy blast from the South Pole. Everything smelled old and unused. I reckon Granny Tuff had bought the furniture from Noah (address, the Ark, Mount Ararat). It was all dark, solid and practical. There was a gigantic wardrobe with big carved handles and doors, and drawers underneath. A huge old-fashioned bed stood against a wall—one of those cast-iron beds that antique dealers would give their eye teeth to buy. The bedspread was a deep red, which my mum calls "maroon". It matched the heavy velvet curtains with bobbles along the hem. The floor was polished dark wood, and there was a maroon-and-cream rug near the bed.

Granny Tuff threw open the wardrobe doors. The overwhelming odour of mothballs had me gasping for breath.

"You can put your things in here," she said.

I tossed everything higgledy-piggledy into the cavernous jaws of the wardrobe. Then I threw my school bag on top of the clothes and shut the doors. Out of sight, out of mind. No way was I going to do any of that homework. What could the principal do to me, anyway? Ground me? Give me detention? Expel me? I was under age: he couldn't chuck me out.

I went back into the kitchen, which was where I thought Granny Tuff had gone. But she wasn't there. I heard the sound of someone chopping wood outside. *Thwack, thwack, thwack.* There was Granny Tuff wielding the axe, chips of wood flying in all directions. Crumbs, she was chopping wood, and she had to be at least seventy!

"You can finish this," she said, putting down the axe.

"Who? *Me?* Forget it," I said.

Granny Tuff stared, then shrugged. "I suppose you don't know how to chop wood."

"No. We've got a gas heater. And a gas stove," I said.

"Never too old to learn," retorted Granny Tuff.

"That's what you think," I shouted rudely. "I will not chop wood."

"No wood, no food," said Granny Tuff.

"Fine. See if I care. I hate scones and puddings and stuff like that."

"No wood, no hot water."

"So?" I sneered. "I'll stay dirty. I won't wash myself and I won't wash my clothes."

"That's your choice," said Granny Tuff calmly.

I stormed back into the house. She couldn't make me do anything I didn't want to do. Granny Tuff wasn't so tough after all. I decided to watch some TV.

There didn't seem to be a television set in the lounge-room. There was just a sofa with carved legs, two matching chairs and an ornate sideboard. On the wall there was a painting of this old geezer who looked a bit like the Grim Reaper ... probably Great-Grandpa Tuff. I'll bet he was a mean old coot. Just as well he wasn't around for this straightening-out process.

I looked in every room, but I couldn't find the TV anywhere. Perhaps Granny Tuff had hidden it. I peered underneath her bed. All I could see was a china chamber-pot with pink roses all over it. I'd never seen a real chamber-pot before. What a giggle!

"What are you looking for, Tina?" said Granny Tuff from the doorway.

"The TV."

"There's no TV."

I gaped. "What? But everyone has a TV."

"No TV, no stereo, no computer, no video," said Granny Tuff. "I don't have any need for these newfangled gadgets."

"No TV!" I couldn't believe it. "What do you do at night?" I asked.

"Read. Knit. Crochet. Write letters."

Boring! I was going to go stark raving mad in this place.

"I won't stay here!" I shouted. "I'll go crazy without TV."

"That could be true," agreed Granny Tuff calmly. "That's your choice."

"My choice?" I yelled. "There is no choice!"

"It's time I peeled the vegetables for the soup," said Granny Tuff.

"You needn't think I'm going to help you peel dumb vegetables for dumb soup," I raged. "I hate vegetable soup."

But I was talking to thin air. Granny Tuff had vanished to the kitchen. I marched into my bedroom. Nothing to do in there. I decided to explore outside.

Around the back of the henhouse I met this black-and-white border collie dog. I liked dogs, although I'd never had one of my own. My real dad had said that the city was no place for a dog, and creepy Mr Donald Donaldson thought dogs were dirty, smelly creatures with fleas.

"Here, boy," I said.

The dog came up to me, wagging his tail. I tickled him behind the ears.

"His name is Sam," said Granny Tuff from behind me. "He was a working dog once, but he's too old now."

I could see that Sam was very old. Everything around here was very old, except me.

I decided to take Sam for a walk. Actually, Sam took me. We went around the front of the house and down a winding gravel road. We walked and walked, but we didn't reach the main road.

I talked to Sam the whole time. "I tell you, Sam, you might like this place, but I hate it," I said to him. "You'd like it in the city, though. There's plenty to do there. And you'd like my gang, the Coucals. You could be our mascot. Of course we really should have a coucal, but they live in Africa. When we get back to the farm I'm going to phone Eva or Zena or Pigman and find out how the Coucals are doing."

I cheered up after that decision. It was beginning to get chilly. Sam turned and began to head back the way we'd come. I guessed that he'd had enough walking for one day.

By the time we got back it was growing dark. Granny Tuff gave me some bones and gravy for Sam. I fed him out on the back veranda. He had a scruffy old rug and a moth-eaten patchwork blanket to sleep on in a corner of the veranda.

"If you came to the city, I'd build you a kennel," I told him. Sam didn't seem very interested in

that idea. He was worn out after his long walk. He flopped down after turning himself around and around, the way dogs do, and went to sleep. I went back to the kitchen.

"Can I use the phone?" I asked Granny Tuff, who was ladling soup out of this big black pot.

"No phone," said Granny Tuff, putting two bowls of soup on the table.

"What? No phone?" I couldn't believe it.

"Eat your soup before it gets cold," said Granny Tuff.

"No way," I yelled, pushing the bowl violently to one side. Soup slopped over the edge and on to the table, but I didn't care.

"I hate vegetable soup. I like tinned tomato soup, or Lots of Noodles," I said angrily. "I won't eat this horrible soup."

"That's your choice," said Granny Tuff, slurping her soup noisily.

"I hate this place, and I hate you!" I yelled, jumping up from the table. "And if you think I'm going to stay here, you're crazy. I'm going to run away, do you hear me?"

Granny Tuff put her spoon down. She looked straight at me with her gimlet eyes. Suddenly I felt scared. I was in the middle of the wilderness with a tough old lady. She could chop me into a million little pieces with that axe of hers, and no one would ever find me. She would say that I'd run away, and everyone would believe her. She could get away with murder!

3

Life on the Farm

I was woken up very early in the morning by this dreadful noise. The rooster was crowing his heart out. What a racket! I looked at my watch. Five-thirty!

I wasn't getting up at five-thirty. No way! I could hear Granny Tuff moving around in her bedroom. Well, I wasn't going to get up until noon!

I'd stormed off to bed the night before without any tea, and in the middle of the night I'd woken up with hunger pangs. I had two Mars bars and a packet of potato chips in my school bag, so I'd eaten those. And half a packet of Steam Rollers I'd found in the pocket of my jeans.

I kept dozing on and off. It was impossible to sleep. Chooks were cackling, a cow was bellowing, Sam barked, and a heap of birds started squawking and fighting right outside my window. Eventually I just had to get up. I couldn't stand it any more. It was only ten o'clock. I decided to have a shower and wash my hair.

The bathroom was at the end of the passage. But where was the shower? There was only a cracked handbasin and an ancient bath perched on these queer clawed iron legs. I'd have a bath, then. I turned on the hot tap. Cold water came out. I waited. Perhaps the hot water took a long time to get through the pipes here. There was this peculiar tank affair at one end of the bathroom. I felt the outside of it. Stone cold. Still there was no hot water.

I went in search of Granny Tuff and found her in the kitchen, drinking tea.

"There's no hot water," I said.

"That would be true," agreed Granny Tuff. "I told you: no wood, no hot water."

I'd told her earlier that I'd stay dirty, but this was yukky. My hair felt like straw. I just had to have a decent wash and shampoo my hair. Granny Tuff looked as if she only washed her hair once a month.

"If you want hot water, you have to split some kindling," she said, "then light up the chip heater in the bathroom. After fifteen minutes, you will have hot water."

She went on drinking her tea.

I was *not* going to chop wood!

I put on my jeans and a windcheater and went outside. There had to be some small pieces of wood around the place. I found an empty cardboard box and began gathering chips, twigs and pieces of bark. When the box was full, I headed back inside. It had taken me nearly an hour to fill the box.

"I guess chopping the wood would have been quicker," I said to Sam, who'd been patiently

26

watching me, "but I will not chop wood. Never, ever!"

I found a little door in the water heater and put in the wood. A box of matches sat on the window-sill. I tried lighting the wood. I'd used up nearly the whole box of matches when finally one little curl of bark caught alight. Soon the fire was blazing merrily. Good. Soon I'd have hot water. I sat on the edge of the bath and kept poking bits of bark and twigs through the little door. Imagine doing this every day of your life, just to get hot water for a bath. This was the pits!

At last hot water came streaming out of the tap into the bath. I felt quite pleased with myself. I, Tina Tuff, had created hot water! I filled the bath right up. I would soak here for hours. After soaping my hair, I lay back and relaxed, until the water started to get cold. I turned on the hot tap. No more hot water! I had to submerge my head quickly to get the shampoo off. At least I was clean. I'd stayed in the bath so long that my skin had wrinkled up like a prune.

By now it was nearly noon. Lunchtime. I was starving. There had to be something decent to eat in this place.

"What's for lunch?" I asked.

"Bread and cheese," said Granny Tuff. "I always eat a light lunch."

"Have you got any peanut butter?"

"No."

"Any Vegemite?"

"No."

"I don't like cheese," I shouted.

"There's jam, honey, lemon spread, marmalade or pickles," said Granny Tuff, "or there's a tin of sardines in the cupboard."

"Old people should eat properly," I said. "We learned that in our health lessons. Old people get malnutrition when they live on bread and cheese."

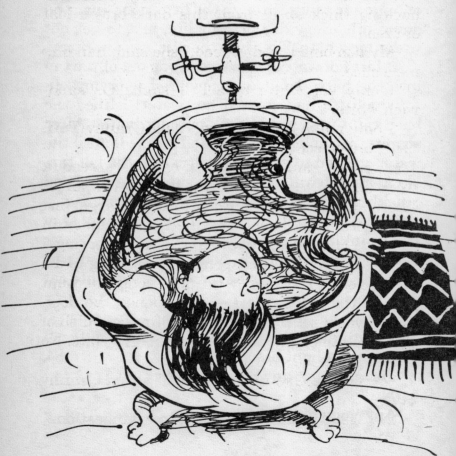

"I have a big meal at breakfast time," said Granny Tuff. "Porridge. Eggs and bacon. Toast and honey. That keeps me going."

"I never eat breakfast," I said. "I don't want to get fat."

"Ah, yes," said Granny Tuff, who would have weighed in at about fifty kilos (with clothes on) if she was lucky, "you don't want to get fat."

I sat down at the table. Granny Tuff was hacking thick slices from this dark brown loaf of bread.

"My homemade soda bread," she said, handing me a slice.

"I only eat white bread," I said. "Oz sandwich white."

"I only make brown bread," said Granny Tuff. "Tuff brown soda."

I was so hungry I didn't care. I spread a thick slice of the dark brown bread with butter (there wasn't any polyunsaturated margarine, was there!) and honey that had gone sugary in the jar. I chewed and chewed. It was like eating a malt-flavoured Wettex sponge. I was going to die of hunger if I stayed here much longer. I went over to the ancient fridge and opened the door. There was a pat of butter, a jug of milk, a dish of thick, yellow cream, and some meat on a plate. No orange juice. No soft drink.

"Would you like a cup of tea?" asked Granny Tuff.

"No," I said sourly. "Tea gives me indigestion."

"There's milk. Or water."

"Water?" I squeaked, as if she'd offered me a cup of poison. Then I had a thought. "Have you any cordial?"

"No. But we could make some from lemons if you like."

Wonderful. I was just hanging out for home-made lemon cordial. I was going to dehydrate if I lived here much longer. And if I drank the water I would probably get some disease.

"That's it," I said. "I can't stay here a moment longer. I'm going, right now."

"You can't go today," said Granny Tuff.

"Why not? Today's as good a day as any," I snapped, heading towards my bedroom.

I grabbed my case from under the bed and started tossing in my clothes. I hauled it back into the kitchen.

"You have a three-mile walk down to the main road," said Granny Tuff. She still talked in miles, not kilometres. "Then there's a two-mile walk to the station. Then you have to wait for the train. It only comes on Mondays and Thursdays."

I stood and gaped at her. I really was a prisoner in this rotten old house! Savagely I dragged my case back and threw my clothes angrily all over the room. All right. She wanted a fight. She'd get one. I'd make her life as miserable as I could. I'd make life so lousy in this dump that she'd beg me to leave!

Then I had another idea. She must have some

sort of transport to the nearest town. She had to get her flour, sugar, meat and fruit from somewhere. I'd get her to take me into town!

I sauntered back out to the kitchen. "I'll just go and chop up a load of wood for you, Granny," I said sweetly.

I walked out the back to the woodshed. I picked up the axe. Only Sam was watching. I held the axe right down low, and pushed the sharp blade hard against my leg until the cloth of my jeans tore and the blade went into my flesh. Blood gushed everywhere.

"Help!" I screamed.

Granny Tuff came bustling out, apron flapping, eyes anxious.

"Oh, oh," I moaned, clutching at my leg, "I've cut myself with the axe. I need a doctor."

Granny Tuff pulled my hand away and peered at the cut. "That could be true," she said, "but there's no doctor for miles. I'll stitch it up." She grabbed me by the elbow. "Come into the house."

"What?" I yelped. "Stitch me up? No way."

Granny Tuff led me to a chair, got some scissors, and cut away my jeans below the knee. My best Levis! I couldn't believe it!

"Those jeans cost fifty-five dollars," I roared. "New acid wash! You've just wrecked my best jeans!"

"Hum," said Granny Tuff. "Cut looks clean. You don't need stitches." She bustled off and came back with this dark brown bottle. "This will sting a bit," she said, and she tipped half the contents on my leg. I nearly went through the ceiling.

"*Eee-oww!*" I roared. I was in agony. It felt like my leg was on fire.

"It won't get infected now," said Granny Tuff happily. "My own antiseptic. Cures anything."

I was nearly fainting with the pain. "Have you ever used it on yourself?" I said through clenched teeth.

"Many times," said Granny Tuff.

I tell you, she was one tough little old lady!

She swaddled my leg in old-fashioned white gauze bandaging, clipping it neatly in place with a safety pin.

"Right," she said. "Now I'll teach you how to chop wood the proper way."

Dazed, I let her lead me outside. My leg was throbbing like mad. If I cut myself at home, Mum would make me lie down for half an hour to counteract the shock. Apparently Granny Tuff didn't believe in shock.

I glanced at her quickly. Was that a humorous glint I'd caught in those shrewd eyes?

She put the axe into my hands. "Put one foot forward, to the side. That's right. Swing the axe from this side. Go on, harder. That's it."

Whack! I hit the wood cleanly, splitting it in two.

"Good. You have a natural ability for chopping wood," said Granny Tuff critically. "You must have inherited it from me."

Good at chopping wood, eh? Natural ability, eh? First time anyone had ever said I was good at anything. Usually people told me how hopeless I was.

"I'll have another go," I said.

Granny Tuff positioned the wood, and stood back. I put my feet in the right position. I lined up the wood. I raised the axe high. *Thwack!* Clean as a whistle, straight through the middle. It was true. I had a natural ability for chopping wood.

I spent the next two hours chopping wood. Not because I had to, mind you, but because I wanted to. No one makes Tina Tuff do anything she doesn't want to do. I really was enjoying chopping this wood. Finally I finished the pile. My shoulders and arms were aching like mad, but I stacked my wood neatly in the shed. I didn't want it getting wet in the evening dew.

While I'd been chopping wood, Granny Tuff had been making pastry. She lined three pie-dishes with the pastry and put them near the open kitchen window, in the cool air.

"I have to milk Moosy now," she said.

Moosy turned out to be a black-and-white cow with a mournful expression and a bulging udder. I had a sudden thought as I stood watching Granny Tuff squirting milk deftly into a bucket.

"Do we . . . use that milk?"

"Yes."

"But it hasn't been pasteurised ... you know ... homogenised ... all that. We could get a disease," I said, horrified.

"Did you hear that, Moosy?" said Granny Tuff indignantly. "Tina thinks your milk is impure. She thinks it has germs in it."

Squish, squish, went the milk into the bucket. Moosy looked reprovingly at me with her doleful cow eyes. I nearly said, "Sorry."

I knew I'd go nuts if I stayed in this place. Not quite two days here, and I was about to apologise to a cow!

I had a sudden thought. "How do you get your grocery supplies, your mail and your papers?" I asked.

"My neighbour, Madge Hobbs, brings me the things I need twice a week."

Ah, a neighbour. Perhaps this Madge could

help me.

"Can we visit Madge tomorrow?" I asked cunningly.

"We could. But she's really too busy to entertain us. She has a sick husband, so she hasn't much time to spare. And it's a fair walk to her place."

"How far?"

"Six miles across country."

Six miles? About ten kilometres? How could I possibly lug my case that far? I'd have to wait until Madge turned up. Then I'd stow away in her car.

"How old is this Madge?" I asked.

"Fortyish."

"Did she know my dad?"

"Sure did. They played in the local band when they were both young and single."

In the local band? A rock group, maybe? Nah, rock music wasn't invented then. Was it? I'd have to ask Madge.

"When does she come?" I asked innocently.

"Day after tomorrow."

Could I stand it until then?

For tea Granny Tuff had made meat pies with mashed potato on top, accompanied by peas and carrots. The pies weren't quite as delicious as shop ones, mind you, and the homemade tomato sauce was different from ordinary sauce, but it all tasted good.

"Would you like a glass of milk?"

I thought of Moosy and all those germs. "Nah. I mean, no thanks. I'll have a glass of water."

Me? Water? I had to be getting desperate.

That night we sat around the table, Granny knitting socks for Red Cross and me with nothing to do. I tried reading a school library book. It was about a gang of kids who got stranded on an island. Perhaps the Coucals could take over an island. There were a few spare ones around Tasmania. No adults. No rules. Cool.

Thinking of the Coucals made me remember William Wormley. Well, he'd been just below the surface of my mind since the accident, but I'd pushed the thought away. My own injured leg was throbbing with a dull pain. Was The Worm in agony? Surely the cops would have come for me if he was dead.

"You got an envelope, Granny?"

No point in writing if we didn't have an envelope.

"Yes. And a stamp. If you want to write letters, Madge will take them to the post office when she comes."

I tore a page out of my school workbook. Mr Dans would chuck a mental. Suffer!

Dear William, I wrote. Too over-the-top. I crossed it out.

Hey, Worm. How are ya? I'm on this farm in the back of nowhere, no phones. I'm sorry about you

*getting hurt. I still don't think you're Coucal
material, but perhaps we can work something
out. So don't die till we talk. Hang loose.*

Tina Tuff

I folded the letter and rammed it in an
envelope. I'd send it to the school 'cos I didn't
know his address.

I should write home, too.

Would I?

Why not?

I tore out another page, and started to write.

Dear Mum, Tommy and Randy,

*The farm is cool. I'm having an unreal time.
Full-on excitement. Don't bother coming back for
me, Mr Donald Donaldson, 'cos I'm gonna live
here forever, marry a farmer, and have ten kids.*

Your former daughter and sister, Tina
XXXXXXXXXXXXXXXXXXXXXXXX

Suffer! See if I cared if they didn't want me.

My eyes were going kind of watery. I must be
over tired, I thought, wiping them with the back
of my hand.

"Time for bed," said Granny briskly. "Tomorrow after lunch I'll take you for a walk right
round the whole farm."

Big deal. I could hardly wait!

4

Tuff Stuff

Walking round the farm *did* turn out to be a big deal, but not in the way I'd expected. The property was huge, and we must have walked hundreds of kilometres. OK, so I'm exaggerating, but to my feet, which were used to civilised footpaths, stumbling over rough grass was agony.

Granny moved like a laser beam straight round the perimeter, yakking happily as she pointed out items of incredible importance to her and incredible boredom to me. Where Maybelle had her first calf, where Boris gored someone, where Lulu had triplets (I figured that Lulu was some kind of animal, but I didn't have enough breath to ask). The rising wind blew her words away as we began the long walk back, so I gave up listening and concentrated on putting one foot in front of the other.

We were half way home when huge icy raindrops began to spatter down. The sky was black and angry. There was going to be one thumping great storm at any minute. Granny Tuff scuttled along, head down, the wind lashing at her coat. My trendy jacket was soaked right through in seconds. Forget looking like a dag; I would have traded it for oilskins now at the drop of a hat. The rain was pouring down in torrents, running right down the back of my neck. We'd tramped across paddock after paddock for hours. They all looked the same to me. Green grass. Fences. An occasional dam. I'd rather be safely at home, warm and dry.

At last we reached the back gate. The hens had all scurried back to the roost. Sam raced up, barking wildly, getting wetter by the minute. The back veranda was saturated from the driving rain, and Sam's bedding was a sodden mess.

"Huh. Easterly," said Granny Tuff. "Haven't had an easterly blow like this for a good five years. It's that hole in the ozone layer."

Sure!

I peeled off my wet clothes in the kitchen, and Granny bustled around banking up the fire in the stove and lighting the open fire in the front room. While I clambered into warm, dry clothes and dried my hair vigorously with a hard white towel (didn't she know about Softly and Comfort, for Pete's sake?), Granny brought Sam in, sat him by the fire, and rubbed his dripping coat with a similar hard white towel. I peered at it closely. I couldn't see "Sam" or "The Dog" written on it anywhere. Oh, yuk. I hoped I wasn't drying my hair with a pre-owned Sam towel. Double yuk!

Granny Tuff spread my clothes and Sam's bedding to dry all round the room, hanging it over strings or draping it across the furniture. The whole place looked like a laundry, with steam rising in great clouds. The air smelled of wet dog and eucalyptus logs. So much for room deodorisers: we had just invented our own brand.

Already it was getting dark outside. I glanced at my watch. Five o'clock. Where had the day gone? Granny appeared from the kitchen with two mugs of hot cocoa. I didn't have enough energy to tell her I was allergic to it. Cocoa brings me out in red, itchy lumps. Heck. Who was here to see a crop of lumps anyway? We sat around the fire, sipping the scalding drinks, while the wind

screamed and howled around the eaves. I prayed that the roof wouldn't blow off. The whole house seemed to be swaying and shaking.

"Don't worry, Tina. This house has been standing for nearly a hundred years," said Granny, noticing my agitation.

Big deal. Even more reason for it to collapse around our ears in a heap of rubble. Then my mum and Mr Donald Donaldson would be *real* sorry. They'd feel guilty for the rest of their lives that I'd got bumped off in my prime, squashed flat under the ruins of a crumbling farmhouse where *they'd* forced me to go! Yeah, guilty for the rest of their lives. I savoured the thought. It would serve them right!

Granny Tuff looked at me and sighed. "I think I know how you feel," she said. "I was like you once ... tough. Smart. A rebel. My father hadn't gone and died on me, but I was still angry about lots of things. Being a girl, for one. I wanted to be like my brothers, mending machinery, baling hay, driving the tractor, but I had to help my mother bottle fruit and bake and do the housework. My dad wanted me to be his little lady, but I wanted to be tough."

"How?" I said. "I mean, how did you be tough? I'm tough because I'm the leader of the Coucals!"

"I was leader of my own gang, too," said Granny.

"Get real," I said. "You? Leader of a gang?"

"Believe it or not," said Granny Tuff.

"I'll tell you about the Coucals if you tell me about your gang," I said cunningly.

"No."

I stared at her. She wasn't interested in the Coucals? Well, then, I wasn't interested in her mouldy old gang either. Between them they probably pinched one lolly out of a milk bar. Big deal.

"Anyway, you're wrong about one thing," I said. "I'm not smart. I'm dumb at schoolwork. I fail everything. And I hate school."

"You only hate school," said Granny Tuff, "because you don't succeed there."

"Who cares?" I said rudely. "Who wants to be brainy, anyway? Boring if you ask me."

"That could be true," said Granny Tuff, "but you've never really given it a chance. What subjects do you like best?"

"Nothing," I said.

Granny Tuff sipped her cocoa and waited.

"I'd like English if I could spell," I said.

"Why can't you look up words in the dictionary?"

"How can I look them up if I can't spell them?" I said angrily.

Granny Tuff got up, went over to the bookshelf, and took down *The Concise Oxford Dictionary*. Dumb name. There was nothing concise about it: it was huge.

"Let's take an example," said Granny Tuff. "'Separate'. It has to start with a 'c' or an 's', doesn't it? Look up 'c-e-p'."

43

"Nah," I said, after looking through all the "c-e-p"s. "Not here."

I tried the "s-e-p"s. "'Separate ...'" I read. "'Physically disconnected, distinct, individual ...'"

"Right," said Granny Tuff. "That's English organised. What about arithmetic?"

She made it sound so simple. It had to be harder than that! "Hang on," I said, "I'll get my maths book. If you can work out decimals you should be President of the National Bank."

Granny Tuff looked at the problems. She checked the answers page at the back. That was nothing wonderful: I always checked the answers at the back. The problem was that I couldn't get the *middle* bit to match the answers!

"It's different from what I learned, but I've figured it out. I'll show you."

When Mr Donald Donaldson had tried to show me, it hadn't made any sense. Now it was easy. I sat doing maths homework with the rain lashing at the windows while Granny made toasted cheese and egg sandwiches in this peculiar thing she called a jaffle iron. Yum. Before I knew it, I'd done three pages of maths problems. I checked the answers. Every sum was right. Unbelievable.

"What else do you need to know?" asked Granny, smiling.

"I need to know about my dad," I blurted out.

"What do you need to know?"

"I dunno." I shrugged. "What he was like when

he was little. That sort of stuff."

"He was easy-going, happy ... popular with all the neighbours."

"Not like Mr Donald Donaldson," I said sourly. "I'll bet he was a real nerd when he was a kid."

"Why don't you like him, Tina?"

"He's a bossy, snobby creep. And he needn't think he can replace *my* father," I shouted, slamming down the maths book. "There's no room for him in my life. I don't trust him!"

"Perhaps you don't really trust yourself," said Granny quietly.

"Aw. What do you know?" I snapped. How could she understand? I'd trusted my dad always to be around, and he'd let me down by dying. I was still angry about that. How dare he die and leave me? I was on my own. Mum and Mr Donald Donaldson had left me here. I couldn't trust my own family. When you trusted people, you got hurt.

I decided to read some more of my book, the one about the gang of kids stranded on a desert island. The leader of the gang was trying to make rules, but everyone was fighting. It was the dumbest book I'd ever read up till now, and I was only half way through it. The leader was a loser because the whole gang was starting to fall apart. One of the boys sounded like Pigman. I always had the feeling that Pigman would like to take over the Coucals. And Zena. I reckoned she'd like to get rid of me too. She often sided with Pigman. The leader of the gang in the book was a wimp. Not like me. If he didn't start getting tough, one of the gang was gonna knock his block off. But still, the book made me think.

"I read that book once," said Granny. She'd left the room, and now she returned clutching something wrapped in a brown cloth bag.

"Good," I said. "You can tell me how it finishes." That would save me wading through the whole book.

"You'll have to read it for yourself," said Granny. "Here. This might be useful for you. It's your dad's old mouth-organ."

Carefully I unwrapped the folds. A silver mouth-organ, once played by my dad. I picked it up, put it to my lips, and blew tentatively. Thin, wispy sounds, little squeaks and squawks, growing more raucous as I blew harder. Yeah, I could get the hang of this. I could play music. Unreal!

"Thanks," I said. "I'm goin' to bed."

My bed was lumpy, unmade from the morning. I wriggled round, unable to sleep, clutching my dad's mouth-organ. Was I mad at him for dying and leaving me, or mad at myself for being afraid, deep down, of loving someone so dearly again? Was that why I acted so tough with my friends? And what about my friends? Would they be loyal to me while I was away? Or would the Coucals now be under the leadership of Pigman and Zena?

Tomorrow was Thursday. If I was going to run away, I'd have to leave early in the morning. Yes,

I'd do it. I was sick and tired of this place. I had
my dad's mouth-organ. What else did I need? I
hadn't found out my dad's entire life story, but
who cared? He was d-e-a-d. Like this hole. I
wanted to be back in the city with the Coucals.

I climbed out of bed and began to shove stuff
into my case, ready to leave. If I lugged it down to
the front gate and hid it in the bushes while it
was pitch black, I could nick out after breakfast,
chuck it in the wheelbarrow with my bag of
books, and rack off to the railway station. And
hope that the train didn't leave at the crack of
dawn. I should've checked with Granny, but then
she'd have become suspicious.

Dragging my case, I opened the bedroom door. I tiptoed past Granny Tuff's room. She was asleep, all right. Rumbling snores filled the silence. Gross. I'd never snore when I got old. The hinges creaked when I opened the front door, but Granny rasping like a chainsaw drowned out the noise.

It had stopped raining. The grass glistened raggedly in the moonlight as I hauled the case down the path and pushed it behind a large bush. I hoped it wouldn't start raining again. Was my case waterproof?

I crept back to bed. Granny was silent. I hoped she hadn't produced an enormous snore and suffocated. Should I check it out? As I was wondering what to do, my hands clasping the mouth-organ, I must have drifted off to sleep.

5

The Escape

Ten o'clock! I couldn't believe it! I'd have to skip breakfast and get something to eat at the railway station. By the time I'd wheeled my case there it would be noon, at least. I wasn't even sure what time the train went.

I scribbled a note to Granny Tuff and left it on my bed. It said: "Thanks for trying, but I have to go back. Love, Tina."

I sneaked down the passage towards the front door. I could hear Granny Tuff rattling around in the kitchen. I would have liked to say goodbye to Sam but it was too risky.

I hurried to the bushes where I'd left my case. I blinked. The case was gone! I searched frantically behind all the bushes along the path. It wasn't there! Some rotten scumbag had stolen my case!

I stormed back into the house. Granny Tuff was seated at the kitchen table with a pile of papers and books scattered about her.

"Did you take my case?" I asked coldly.

"No."

"I left it out the front by the bushes, and it's gone," I snapped. "A case can't just disappear into thin air."

"That's true," said Granny Tuff serenely.

"Where is it? Do you know?"

"My friend Madge took it."

"Where?" I said, trying not to lose my temper.

"To the railway station."

My mouth dropped open with shock. This Madge had taken my case to the railway station? It didn't make sense.

where's
my case?

"If you change your mind, she'll check at the station and bring it back with the groceries this afternoon."

"Good one," I said crossly. "Why couldn't Madge have taken me, too? Now I have to walk for hours."

"You were sound asleep," Granny Tuff pointed out, "and you have plenty of time to walk there.

The train doesn't leave until two o'clock."

"You're not supposed to let me run away," I spluttered. "Aren't you going to try to stop me? I'm only eleven."

"No," said Granny Tuff. "You can go if you want to, or stay if you want to. You are not a prisoner."

Well, that was news to me. I thought I was supposed to stay at this rotten old farm until I rotted away into nothing.

"You're not mad at me for going?"

"No."

"You're not feeling bad because you've failed with me?"

"No."

"Well, perhaps I'll have some toast and jam before I go," I said, relieved. I made my toast, buttered it thickly, and spread it with a layer of dark plum jam. Granny Tuff's attention was back on her papers.

"Look at this," she said, waving this paper under my nose. I looked. It appeared to be part of an essay, rows and rows of Granny Tuff's neat copperplate handwriting. A large D was written at the top in red biro.

"I'm studying Australian History at the university. I'm a mature age, off campus student," she explained.

Granny Tuff a uni student? Was I hearing right?

"Aren't you a bit old to be at the uni?" I asked

52

incredulously.

"There are people older than I am doing the course. One man is eighty-two."

"That's crazy," I said. "Who'd want to employ someone with a degree at eighty-two?"

Granny Tuff laughed. "We're not studying for a degree to get a job," she chuckled. "It's because most of us had to leave school when we were twelve and go to work to help support our families. It was the time of the Great Depression. Now we have an opportunity to study and to learn."

"Leave school at *twelve*?" I gasped. "Boy, that you could be so lucky! Fifteen is the official leaving age, and I can't wait!"

"Well, it was twelve in those days. Merit Certificate."

"Yeah? Well, I'd like to get hold of the twerp who put the age up to fifteen," I raged. "I'd wring his neck."

Granny Tuff shrugged and began reading some comments written on an official-looking page.

"Anyway, you may as well chuck it in," I said sarcastically. "You only got a D."

"D stands for Distinction," said Granny Tuff.

Wow. A Distinction! I looked at her in awe. She was quite a brainy old bird!

"I gained a High Distinction for this other essay."

Double wow! I was related to a genius!

"I wish I could leave school right now, for ever,

and never go back," I said.

"I thought that was why you wanted to go back to the city?"

"No. I want to see how the Coucals are doing. You know, my gang."

"Oh."

"I told you, I hate school. It's full of nerds and suck-ups, and teachers who give me a hard time."

"That could be true."

"You are cool," I said admiringly, "but I have to go and catch this train. Thanks for trying to help me, but I think I'm beyond it. Goodbye, Gran."

I bent and kissed her cheek.

"Goodbye, Tina. Good luck," she said.

I went out and gave Sam a big hug. I could feel tears prickling at the back of my eyelids. Time to go before I made a fool of myself.

I set off down the road, carrying my school bag. I should have put it with the case: it was heavy enough to be a nuisance.

Granny Tuff had to be the most amazing person I'd ever met. She didn't fuss. She didn't nag. She hadn't set any rules for me about making my bed or doing my washing (which meant that my case was full of dirty clothes). Yet I'd felt secure there at her house, learning to eat her funny food, learning to chop wood, make hot water, bank the fire . . . And she was letting me go back home on the train without trying to talk me out of it! She hadn't even offered me the train fare. I guess she figured that if I was going to catch a train I had money! Maybe she thought that was *my* problem. I was truly sorry to be leaving, but I was also anxious to get back with the Coucals before they forgot me. That was scary.

I kept on trudging down the winding gravel track. Eventually it joined up with the main road, which was still gravelly, pitted with potholes and corrugations. No cars came along. The paddocks were flat and seemingly endless, studded with munching beef cattle wearing browny-red-and-white coats. Herefords, Granny Tuff had told me: prime beef on the hoof. It almost put me off meat for life.

I had a sudden thought. When I came to the main road, I had turned left automatically. What if the railway station was in the other direction? There were no signs. I didn't even know the name of the nearest town. How dumb can you be? What should I do, keep walking and hope that I found the station? Or should I go back the other way?

I squinted. There seemed to be a sign up ahead. I hurried on, changing my bag from one shoulder to the other. Stupid bag, I should throw it over the nearest fence. Who needed school-books anyway?

The sign read "Weerinoma, 4 km". Good one. Was the railway station there or not? I'd have to take a punt. I'd never even heard of Weerinoma—probably it was some little one-horse town out here in the middle of the mulga. I hoped they sold burgers and Coke there. I should have just

55

enough money after paying my train fare. If I didn't have enough, I'd sneak on the train and do a crying act at the other end. Then I'd get a taxi home . . .

Finally, just as I thought it must be forty kilometres to Weerinoma and not four, I saw some buildings in the distance. I increased my pace. It was already one o'clock. If the railway station wasn't here, I'd have to hoof it back at full speed.

As I entered the township I could see the station at the far end of a group of buildings. I heaved a sigh of relief. Now for something to eat.

Weerinoma seemed to consist of a general store, a church, a garage and a pub. All the buildings looked as if a strong wind would blow them over: they were all built of weathered wood, like Granny Tuff's place. Perhaps they'd never heard of paint here!

I trudged into the general store.

"You must be Granny Tuff's girl," said this bent old geezer who was serving at the counter. News travels fast around these parts. I'd barely left her place!

"Do you have any hamburgers?" I asked hopefully.

The old man rummaged in a battered freezer and produced a packet of frozen burgers. Sure! How was I supposed to cook them?

"I meant a cooked hamburger," I explained.

He nodded, opened the packet, and shuffled out the back. I looked around. What could I nick? No one was watching. I reached out towards the chocolate bars. Then I stopped myself. What if it got back to Granny Tuff that I'd pinched stuff from this old guy's shop? Her name would be mud. And he'd make her pay for it. I withdrew my hand. The smell of hamburger wafted through the air, sizzling away with onions. Yum. My mouth was watering.

"Hey," I yelled, "I'll have lettuce, no tomato, no cheese, no egg, and double bacon, double sauce."

There was no reply. I shifted from one foot to the other. Perhaps the old coot had dropped dead out there. It was taking forever.

To while away the time, I studied the store. The sagging shelves held an assortment of groceries—tins of soup, jelly crystals, cordial, coffee, biscuits, detergents and flour, all jumbled together. On the front counter were rows of large glass jars labelled "Boiled lollies", "Acid drops", "Humbugs", "Butterscotch", "Rainbow balls", "Aniseed balls" ... I'd never heard of half these lollies. Black squares labelled "Licorice blocks" looked interesting; perhaps I'd buy a handful to see what they were like.

The old dude shuffled out with my burger wrapped in greaseproof paper.

"How much?" I asked.

"One dollar," he said, almost apologetically.

"One dollar?" I gaped. Inflation hadn't caught up here. I'd been going to have a Coke, but perhaps I'd get a better deal with a milkshake.

There was heaps of milk around these parts, wasn't there? "How much for a milkshake, double chocolate?"

"And malt?"

"Yeah." Why not?

"Eighty cents," said the old man. He reached for this silver container. I hadn't seen one of those since I was tiny. He poured in lots of milk, two overflowing ladles of chocolate syrup, and a *full* scoop of vanilla icecream. Then he tipped in a huge spoonful of malt, and clipped the container under the machine. I tell you, that milkshake was so enormous it was nearly spilling over the edges of the container. He put it, together with an old-fashioned glass, on the top of the counter.

Where was I supposed to drink this milkshake? I couldn't see any tables or chairs. I couldn't take the glass and container with me: the store didn't cater for take-away milkshake drinkers.

Just outside the door, facing the main street, I found an old wooden bench. This must be where milkshake drinkers were supposed to sit. Perhaps my dad sat here once, long ago. I unwrapped my burger. Wouldn't you know? He'd given me tomato, cheese and egg as well as everything else. And all for a dollar! You could live on the poverty line in this joint!

I ate my hamburger, sipped my milkshake and looked at the passing traffic, which was easy. There was none! Being seated on a bench outside the general store in Weerinoma was not a breath-

taking experience. And it was cold. It looked as though it might start to rain. This had to be the wettest, coldest place in Australia.

I finished off the milkshake and took the container back inside, leaving it on the counter. There was no sign of the old man. I hoped he hadn't carked it out the back.

I set off for the station. I wanted to be in plenty of time to buy my ticket. I couldn't stand being in this place until Monday, which was when the next train would come if I missed this one.

The station was closed when I arrived, and there was a sign on the office door saying "Back at 1.30". I looked at my watch. It was twenty past one. Everything moved so slowly in this town. Probably the Station Master had nicked off home for a hot lunch.

Standing on tiptoe, I just managed to peer through the dusty window. Against the wall I could see my suitcase. Phew! That was one less worry. There were stacks of parcels, crates and boxes waiting to be loaded on to the train. So long as there was room for me, who was caring?

The silence was broken by the sound of a car approaching. The Station Master, no doubt. A white Holden drew up, and this skinny old man clambered out. Weren't there any young guys in this town? So far I hadn't seen one person under seventy! I could write a horror story about this, and flog it off to one of those science fiction magazines. Or even to TV. "The Living Legend of the Dismal Dead". Perhaps they were mutants from outer space, and the general store was a tracking station in disguise ...

"Can I help you, miss?"

I jumped about two metres in the air. The Station Master was looking at me quizzically. Then he clapped a hand to his head. "You must be

Granny Tuff's granddaughter. Come in, come in."

He produced a bunch of keys, fumbled, selected one, and inserted it into the lock. How come everyone knew who I was? Granny Tuff hadn't pinned a notice on the back of my coat, had she? I twisted around to look. I couldn't see any note. Perhaps they were all clairvoyant or something. Nothing would surprise me in this one-horse town.

I had to wait while he unlocked another door, then some drawers, then the till. I was leaning against the counter, ready to buy my ticket.

Suddenly I felt anxious. What was I going back to? Obviously they didn't want me at home. I squared my shoulders. OK, so I'd be a street kid and live in a Vin Bin. Or maybe the Coucals would share me around from house to house. I'd been so eager to leave that I'd forgotten *what* it was like at home, at school, in the city.

Huh. I was getting soft. I had to be strong. Tough Tina Tuff.

"Are you Tina?"

A fat, anxious looking woman with wobbly chins rushed up, panting with the effort of moving her bulk at a fast trot.

"What's up?" I didn't like fat ladies I didn't know grabbing at my arm.

"I'm Madge, Granny Tuff's friend. The doctor just phoned me. Your granny's taken a bit of a turn."

A bit of a turn? What was this? And how did

61

Fat Madge know?

As if she could read my mind, Madge said, "She has an emergency beeper which connects directly to the doctor's surgery. He phoned me. It's her heart."

Beeper? Heart? I went cold all over. I picked up my suitcase and followed Madge on wobbly legs out to her old car. Vaguely I heard a toot as the train pulled into the station. Too bad. Next time.

Madge started the car. What a crate. We trundled down the road doing all of forty kilometres an hour.

"Can't you go any faster?" I asked.

"No."

Madge was a person of few words. I bit my lip as we neared Granny Tuff's farm. I was out of the car and running before Madge had hit the brakes. Through the front door I sped, down the passage and into the kitchen, my heart pounding with fear.

Granny Tuff was sitting at the kitchen table, drinking a cup of tea!

6

Conned

I stopped, flabbergasted.

"Granny," I said.

I rushed over and put my arms around her. "You should be lying down," I said. "Come on, I'll help you to your room."

There was the sound of another car pulling up outside.

Madge appeared in the doorway, followed by an elderly man carrying a black bag. The doctor! Did everyone have one foot on a banana skin and the other in the grave around here? I was caught in a time warp, a world of old people.

"She told me you were dying," I said, pointing accusingly at Madge, while Granny gazed sheepishly from Madge to the doctor and back again.

"And I received a beep from your machine," said the doctor.

Had she been faking to get me back?

The doctor was bending over Granny. He looked stern.

"She's all right," I said crossly. "She's sitting here, as fit as a fiddle, drinking tea!"

"Ah, yes ... but I did have a bit of a turn," said Granny.

"And you haven't been in to get your prescription filled for those heart pills, have you?" said the doctor severely, listening to her heartbeat with his stethoscope. "Granny, will you stop drinking tea while I'm examining you?"

Granny set her lips in a thin line. I looked at her. I recognised that look. That's what *I* always did when someone was annoying me.

"Has Granny got something wrong with her heart?" I asked. How could someone have a heart problem when they could zip around paddocks at the speed of light and wield an axe like an Amazon? Granny Tuff had to be the healthiest person I knew.

"Yes," said the doctor curtly. "It's getting older, wearing out."

"Oh," I said, stunned.

The doctor produced a phial of pills. "Tina, you must make sure your grandmother has one of these pills morning and night, before meals."

Great. Now I had to hang about to look after Granny Tuff! Why couldn't Madge move in? If she didn't volunteer ... She didn't. Some friend, huh. So, if I didn't stay and make sure she swallowed these pills every day, she'd probably forget, and cark it right here on the kitchen floor. Then guess who'd be feeling guilty for the rest of her entire life? That's right. Me.

"All right," I said. "I'll stay. But in the meantime," I went on, glaring at Granny, "you are going to fill out an application form to get the phone connected."

Granny opened her mouth to protest. Her beady little eyes flashed angrily. She did not want the phone connected.

"Hey. When I get back home I'll phone you every day," I said cajolingly. "I'll tell you about the Coucals and about Randy and Tommy. And you can tell me about Sam, and Moosy, and the chooks." I just knew who was going to have the most exciting news.

Granny sighed. Then she gave a small nod.

Victory! Now I'd really committed myself. I'd have to phone her every day once I got home. Tina Tuff always keeps her word.

We made Granny lie down on her bed, and then the doctor left, and Madge went to collect the groceries, promising to return as soon as she could. Big deal.

The doctor had said he'd pull strings to get the phone on as soon as possible. At least we had the beeper to use if there was an emergency. I felt a bit scared—an eleven-year-old kid alone with an old woman on a farm in the middle of nowhere ...

Suddenly I didn't feel so tough. I bit my lip. Then I straightened my shoulders. I had work to do. I went outside to milk Moosy. First of all she wouldn't go into the cow bail for me. Finally I coaxed her in with half a bale of hay, and got a rope around her hind legs; I didn't quite trust her not to kick me. I'd watched Granny Tuff extracting litres of milk from Moosy with the greatest of ease, her fingers moving effortlessly. I just didn't have the touch. I pulled and tugged and squeezed with all my might, managing to get only a few pathetic dribbles. What on earth was I going to do? Moosy had to be milked or she'd blow up and burst.

"Please, Moosy," I begged.

Then I started to cry, great hacking sobs. Me, Tina Tuff, bawling like a sooky baby!

Swish. Swish. I couldn't believe it. Moosy, feeling sorry for me, was letting down her milk.

"Thanks, Moosy, old girl," I said, kissing her rough furry side.

What else? I had to collect the eggs. Feed the chooks and make sure they were safe for the night. Bring in some wood. Then I gathered piles of washing off the line. Granny Tuff had washed all my bedlinen and my towels. She must have thought I'd gone for good. Well, hadn't I? I felt guilty. What if the heavy washing had been too much for her? What if that had brought on her "turn"?

I staggered inside and started draping the washing all over the clothesline and the furniture.

A car! Thank God. Madge! She bustled inside with bags of groceries, papers and the mail.

"I'd stay with you, Tina, but I have an invalid husband to care for, and four children to look after ..."

I felt terrible. I'd forgotten about Madge's sick husband. I'd thought she was just a fat blob of

lard, and she had all these problems to contend
with in her own family, let alone Granny Tuff.

"I'll be fine," I said. "And thank you for taking
my case this morning. And for bringing me back.
And for being such a good friend to my gran."

My gran. That sounded . . . good.

"You've got the beeper, Tina. The doctor can
be your contact. He'll phone me if needs be and
I'll come straight over. Oh, there's two letters
for you."

Two letters? But mine had just been posted
this morning. There was no time for replies.

I opened the first letter.

Dear Tina,

We miss you and hope everything is going well ... (There was more news about the washing-machine packing up, Mr Jones' milk bar being robbed, other local stuff.) ... *The place isn't the same without you, Tina. We've decided that Don will pick you up on Sunday week. We all send our love and kisses.*

Mum, Don and the boys
XXXXXXXX

Huh!
The other envelope had wobbly, spidery writing.

Dear Tina,

Sorry I made you get into trouble. I only have two cracked ribs. I guess I'm not tough enough to join the Coucals. But I don't want to anyway. They are turning BAD. Sorry again.

William

He was sorry? *I* was the one to be sorry! At least he wasn't dead. But what was this about the Coucals turning bad? That was nuts. The Coucals were wild, we were rebels, but we weren't bad. Oh, well, I'd sort it out when Don came for me on Sunday. Hey, I'd called him "Don". Huh! Hey, perhaps he wouldn't come when they got my letter saying I wanted to stay. What a mess!

I glanced at the clock. Five-thirty. Oh, no. I'd have to cook the tea. Me, Tina Tuff, the world's worst cook! It wasn't my fault that I hadn't learned yet. What could I cook so that whatever I did to it we could still eat it?

Stew! That was easy. You just bunged in meat and vegetables and cooked it. But it took hours to make stew. We wouldn't eat until eight o'clock. What, then? Sandwiches? Jaffles?

I looked in the fridge. There was some cooked rissole mince in a bowl. I tasted it. Curry! Good. And also on the shelf was an apple pie. I put the curry into a saucepan and the pie into the oven.

Thank heavens the fire was still going in the stove. But how hot should it be? I tried to remember what Granny did. She was always shoving wood into it and doing something with a lever on the side. I grabbed the poker and lifted the lid to peer inside. Glowing embers. It probably needed more wood. I brought in an armful, opened the door and stuffed in as much as I could. I gave it several minutes, then peered in again. It wasn't even smouldering. I gave it a poke. Now what? The lever! I opened it wide, and that was like waving a magic wand, because the wood began to glow and then to crackle. Soon I had an enormous fire blazing. Was it too hot? Could it melt the chimney? I closed the lever and the fire died down, although it still burned away merrily. I looked at the pie. Horrors, the top was going black!

I pulled it out, forgetting that the pie plate would be hot, and managed to burn my hand! This was awful. If I could have phoned for pizza with the lot, I'd have done it! I scraped off the burnt bits and then, hoping the oven had cooled off a bit because I'd left the door open, I shoved the pie back in and closed the door. The curry was boiling like a volcano about to erupt. I moved the pot to one side like I'd seen Granny do. This was the pits. What else could I make that wouldn't burn or explode?

Rice. I could make boiled rice to go with the curry. But how did you cook rice? How much did you need for two people? I got a big pot, half filled it with water, and poured in a packet of rice. It didn't look much, but that was all the rice there was. I'd have to spread it on the plates, make it look like there was lots.

The doctor had said it was important to keep Granny warm. I checked on her again, fed Sam, and put some more wood on the parlour fire. Then I went back into the kitchen. My eyes widened in horror. The rice had swollen right over the top of the pot and down the sides. It had expanded until I had enough for twenty people! Stupid stuff. I whipped the pot off the stove and headed out the back door.

"Here, Sam! Extra food!" I put some rice in his bowl, and Sam sniffed at it cautiously. Did rice kill dogs? Would it swell in his tummy and blow him into a zillion pieces? This was horrible! I took the rest of the rice back inside.

"You've got enough there for a dozen people," said Granny from the doorway.

"Granny! You should be in bed!"

"Nonsense. I feel fine."

"Well, sit down here quietly, and I'll dish up your tea," I said. "No. Here by the fire. Are you warm enough? Do you want your rug?"

"For goodness sake, stop fussing, girl. I tell you, I'm fine."

I ladled out the contents of both pots. Granny ate all her food, a good sign. I was ravenous. This stuff was quite tasty. Perhaps I should actually learn how to cook.

"We can use the extra rice for a baked custard tomorrow," said Granny, when I went to toss it in the chooks' pail.

"How?"

"Like you make an egg flip. You beat eggs into two cups of milk and add a tablespoon of sugar and a few drops of vanilla. Whisk it all up and you have egg flip or custard to bake."

That sounded simple.

After tea I washed and dried the dishes, then got out my homework. Without TV to distract me I was able to concentrate. I zoomed through another four pages.

"You are really getting good at your maths," said Granny, pleased. It was the first time since I was in Prep that anyone had told me I was good at maths! I felt great.

"Tell me more about my dad," I said, once we'd settled around the stove to keep warm.

"What sorts of things would you like to know?"

"What he did when he lived here with you and Grandpa. The things he did in the evenings. Who his friends were."

"Well, you knew he had a brother, your Uncle Ken."

"Yes. he lives in Queensland. We never see him."

"Your dad and Ken liked to go exploring up in the mountains."

"So he was the adventurous type," I said with pride.

"He'd have a go at anything," replied Granny Tuff, "but not all outdoors. He liked reading. And he loved playing his mouth-organ, especially in the band."

"With Madge!" I remembered. "What did she play, the drums?"

Granny Tuff pretended to look shocked. "Girls didn't play the drums in those days," she said. "They mostly played the piano. Madge was a real twinkle-fingers."

Madge! Who cared about Madge? I wanted to hear that my dad had played the hottest mouth-organ in the whole of Australia.

"So what was the band called?" I asked impatiently.

"Silver Linings."

What a dumb name! I'll bet my dad had a real radical name to call it, like "Wanton Warriors" or "Murder Magnates" or "Meltdown Monarchs", and the others had out-voted him. Betcha!

"Where did the Silver Linings play?" I said. "Did they cut a record? Did they make a video?"

Granny chuckled. "Record? Video? Of course not! They played at the local dances on Saturday nights down at the church hall."

Huh! Betcha if they'd had a decent pianist and a decent drummer and a decent guitarist and a decent *name* they would've been world famous!

"What else did Dad do?" I asked.

"His favourite hobby was mending things— farm machinery, tinkering around with engines. He could get any old rusty engine, take it apart, clean it up, and get it going again. He'd fix up cars for the folk around here."

"He liked it here on the farm?"

"Yes. He was happy on the farm and happy in his work. Then he met your mother. She was a city girl—she wouldn't live on the farm."

"So they lived in the city," I said, feeling angry at my mother.

"He was happy enough," said Granny Tuff, as if she knew what I was thinking. "Your mother would have pined out here in the country. It all worked out for the best."

Like me. I was pining for the Coucals. Or was I?

7

Going Home

The days flew by. I had my chores to do—wood-chopping, milking, house-cleaning, walks with Sam, meals to prepare (I was working my way through the cookbook), my schoolwork to do, the farm to check on daily ... and Granny Tuff. She seemed much better. The phone line was being brought from the main road and would be connected soon. Madge had become a good friend, and popped in when she could. She'd told me lots of great stories about when my dad was at school, and she'd also taught me to blow a mean tune on the mouth-organ: when she and Dad were kids, they'd played duets.

One afternoon I was in the kitchen finishing off an essay for Mr Dans when a car door slammed outside. Who could be visiting? It wasn't Madge's day for deliveries. I hurried to the front door. And there stood Mr Donald Donaldson on the doorstep. I'd forgotten: it must be Sunday, and time for me to go home! I'd lost track of time.

"Hi," I said, smiling broadly. "Come on in." I led the way down to the kitchen. "I'll just call Granny," I said. "She's in the vegie garden."

When I returned with Granny in tow, my stepdad was reading the essay I'd been writing. He looked up guiltily, then noticed that I wasn't mad.

"Tina," he said, "did you write this?"

I nodded.

"It's very good," he said.

"Granny helped me with writing English," I said. "And maths. And heaps of other things."

"That's fantastic," he said, sounding pleased.

I made a pot of tea, and put the Anzac biscuits I'd made the day before on to a plate.

"Yum," said my stepdad, biting into an Anzac. "Nothing like home cooking."

"As made by Tina," said Granny.

"*You* made these?" He looked at me as if a revelation had taken place. "Is this really you, Tina Tuff?"

"Hey," I said, "let's get one thing straight here. I have changed, but not *that* much. I still get angry, I still think lots of things are stupid, I still keep my room untidy, and I still hate doing my washing. OK?"

Mr Donald Donaldson laughed. "It would be boring if you changed too much, Tina."

"That could be true," agreed Granny.

"Listen," I said to my stepdad, "I've been thinking. I know you want me to call you Dad, but I can't. It just doesn't feel right. Could I call you Don?"

"Sure, Tina. That sounds fine."

It would take some getting used to, calling him Don when I'd never called him anything before (except swearwords under my breath!).

I said goodbye to Sam, and to Moosy, and finally to Granny Tuff.

Granny took both my hands. "Tina," she said, "you have a reputation among your city friends for being tough. It will be hard to live down. Give a dog a bad name, and it will stick. But remember this. You will always be able to be anything you want or do anything you want if you believe in yourself. If you are responsible for your own feelings and needs, no one can ever put you down or hurt you. It's called 'inner strength'. That's the true meaning of tough."

I hugged her tightly. "I'll be back in the next holidays," I promised, my eyes blurred with tears. "Thank you, Granny Tuff."

Finally we arrived back home. Mum was glad to see me, and we didn't get into any arguments, although she wanted to gossip about Granny Tuff and what she called her eccentric ways. In the end she gave up quizzing me. Tommy had gone out, and Randy didn't want to talk 'cos he was watching TV. No one would think that I'd been away. I might as well have been a fly on the wall. But I didn't get mad or sulky. If they didn't want to talk, that was their problem, not mine.

Don and I hadn't had any tea, although we'd stopped at a roadside café for a snack. Mum phoned a dial-a-pizza place and ordered a large pizza with the lot. I wandered out into the kitchen and made myself an egg-and-banana milk flip to have with the pizza. Then it was time for bed.

Monday. Back to school. I humped my school bag in through the gate. I'd barely got inside the grounds when Mr Creedy came racing up and grabbed me by the arm.

"Into the principal's office, Tina Tuff."

Now what? Was this the welcoming committee? As we walked down the corridor I was shocked. Someone had vandalised the school. There were torn books everywhere, graffiti all over the walls. What a mess.

There were two cops in the office, talking to the principal and Mr Dans. They stopped talking as I was propelled through the door.

"Tina Tuff," said the principal. He was white with rage. "Your gang is responsible for this outrage."

My mouth dropped open with shock. I couldn't believe it. The Coucals had done all this damage? It was absurd!

"I didn't do it," I said firmly.

One of the things I'd learned from Granny Tuff was that it was important to stick to your guns. She called it being assertive. I knew that I must

not get sidetracked into defensive explanations. I was innocent.

"Two of the Coucals have admitted that you organised this terrible act," said the principal. "You have gone too far this time, Tina Tuff."

Through my shock, I remembered Granny Tuff's words. *Give a dog a bad name.* That's what she had warned me about. But why had the Coucals lied about me?

"Where were you last night?" asked one of the cops.

"I was travelling back from my granny's farm with my stepfather," I said. "We had a snack at the roadside café at Bunkers Hill at seven o'clock."

"And then?"

"I was at home with my family. At nine o'clock I took delivery of a pizza at the front door."

"And then?"

"I went to bed."

"She probably climbed out the window," snapped the principal. "I know she is involved in this vandalism. It's high time she had a spell in a detention centre. It might teach her a lesson."

Nice!

"Why would your friends say you were involved?" asked Mr Dans.

"I don't know," I replied, looking him squarely in the eye. "I didn't do it."

"She's telling the truth," said the cop. And I'd always thought cops had no brains!

"Thank you," I said with dignity.

The principal didn't look too sure. I guess my track record was swaying his judgement. I needed a real friend more than I'd ever needed one before in my whole life. But who in this whole school would want to be seen as my friend? They'd have to be as tough as ... as a Coucal!

"You can leave," said the principal sourly. "And let this be a lesson to you."

It was. It was. Don't trust your so-called friends!

Mr Dans walked to the door with me. The first person I saw was The Worm, propping up the passage wall. His face was grim. He stepped forward in front of Mr Dans.

"Sir."

"Yes, Wormley?"

"Tina didn't do it," he blurted.

"So who did, Wormley?"

Would he dob? The Coucals would get him for sure. I shook my head warningly. The Worm shut his eyes and swallowed. Then he looked straight at Mr Dans.

"It was Pigman and Zena, sir. I saw them."

"Pigman?"

"Pete Kildarney."

"Into the principal's office, Wormley."

First day back at school, in trouble for something I hadn't done. My friends had betrayed me. Pigman and Zena. I'd had bad vibes and my instincts had been right. What about the other Coucals? Did they still want to hang around with me? And how about The Worm, sticking up for me? He sure wasn't a worm after all. I headed for the Grade 6 room. It was time to help clean up all the mess.

When I saw Zena and Pigman being taken down the corridor with the cops, I turned my back. How could I ever have thought those two were my friends?

During the break Rod, Ben and Ziggie, Sharon, Lisa, Frankie and Eva came up to me sheepishly.

"Hi, Coucals," I said. I tried to sound casual, but my heart was pounding.

"Sorry, Tina."

"Yeah. Pigman and Zena took over the gang. It was fun at first."

"Yeah. Wild."

"But then they wanted us to break into cars," said Ziggie.

"Yeah. And wreck people's letterboxes, steal their mail," said Lisa. "We don't want them in the gang any more."

"Yeah. We want *you* as leader again, Tina," said Rod, scuffling his sneakers in the dirt.

"I'll only be the leader on one condition," I said.

"What?"

"William Wormley joins the Coucals."

"Huh? The Worm?"

"Yeah. He's the only one who had the guts to stick up for me, to dob in Pigman and Zena."

"The principal wouldn't believe us when we tried to tell him," whined Lisa.

"Well, Mr Dans believed The Worm, and seeing as the cops have got Pigman and Zena, it looks like the principal believed him, too," I said. "So William Wormley is now a Coucal and not a Worm! Got it?"

"Yeah, yeah, yeah."

"No problem with me."

"Cool."

The Coucals don't do so much hooning around nowadays. We hang out at the milk bar a bit, and in William's garage, 'cos we're starting a hot

rock group, the Cool Coucals. Lisa and Eva don't play instruments, so they're doing the posters and the PR, and we let them bang a couple of tambourines occasionally. Ziggie and Rod are on guitars, Sharon's doing vocals, Ben's on the drums and Frankie's on keyboard. It's a bit rough, but when I blast away on the mouth-organ it sounds hot.

One night I phoned Granny Tuff and we played two of our numbers straight into the receiver, which William held. We all had a quick yak. I give her a ring every night just to make sure she's

taken her pills, and she's doing fine.

Granny thinks the Cool Coucals are going to be a huge success, and if we hit TV she's even going to buy a set!

I know we'll make it big one day.

Why?

'Cos William Wormley is our manager!

And Tina Tuff is *tough*.

Glossary

Cark it: die (shortened form of carcass)

Chook: chicken

Dag: a slovenly, untidy, tacky person. Can be used affectionately, as can most Australian insults, for an eccentric, odd or amusing person (comes from 'dags', the unpleasant wool around a sheep's bottom!)

Dob: tell on, inform against

Hoon: an aggressive or surly youth, or to drive fast and recklessly

Jocks: underpants

Mulga: bush, outback

Punt: risk, gamble (as in 'take a punt')

Rack off: leave, go away (form of abuse)

Sooky: cowardly, cry-baby

Steam Rollers: famous brand of white mint-flavoured sweets

Vin Bin: St Vincent de Paul large clothing collection bin left in the streets for the public to place donated clothing. (St Vincent de Paul is a Catholic charity organisation)